The Adventures of
Maya and Grampa

Kenneth L. Marshall

ISBN 0-7414-2016-3

Published by:

INFINITY
PUBLISHING.COM
1094 New Dehaven Street
Suite 100
West Conshohocken, PA 19428-2713
Info@buybooksontheweb.com
www.buybooksontheweb.com
Toll-free (877) BUY BOOK
Local Phone (610) 941-9999
Fax (610) 941-9959

Printed in the United States of America
Printed on Recycled Paper
Published June 2004

MAYA

This book is dedicated to "My Best Friend Ever," Maya.

Maya is a little girl who just happened to be born in China but her mission in life was to turn a bitter old man into a loving "Grampa."

Maya was adopted by Marla Lewellyn in 1998 and taken to the city of Greensboro, North Carolina when she was approximately thirteen months old. She came into "Grampa's" life immediately after Christmas time that year.

I, being "Grampa," fell in love with her quite by accident. It was not intentional and it was not pre-ordained or planned. It just happened when I looked into those huge wet black eyes for the first time. I could see clear to her soul and I fell head over heels in love. At the age of three, she looked up at me one day while we were working in the garage and said, "Grampa, you are my berry bestest friend ever." I have never forgotten that honest statement made by a tiny girl with huge wet black eyes.

From 1998 until her mother passed away in July of 2001, Maya and I became inseparable. When I lost my oldest son Steven in 1999, I was convinced the Lord had sent her to fill the void. She named me "Gampy Poo" as we read the Winnie the Pooh series and when she asked me to write her a book, Maya and "Gampy Poo" were just natural characters. So begins the Stories of Maya and Gampy Poo. We hope you enjoy them.

Gampy Poo
Grampa
Ken

Chapter One

The Deep Dark Rabbit Hole

Once upon a time there was a little girl named Maya who lived in a beautiful castle in The Enchanted Forest.

Her very best friend ever was an old Grampy Poo.

Now everyone knows that a Grampy is a Grampa, and a Poo is an old yellow bear who wears a red shirt.

So Maya's best friend ever was an old Grampa Bear and they did everything together.

One day when Grampy Poo was walking through The Enchanted Forest, he fell into a hole dug by Maya's friend, Rabbit.

Old Grampy Poo was very frightened because it was dark inside this deep old hole and he started to yell: "Maya, Maya, someone get Maya! She is the only one who will know how to get me out of this hole. Please hurry. It is dark down here."

Maya's old friend Hoot The Owl was flying overhead. He heard Grampy Poo yell for help and he just had to stop and find out what had happened.

2

Owl landed on the edge of the hole and peering down into the dark said, "Whooooo, Whooooo's down there in this deep dark rabbit hole?"

From the hole came Grampy Poo's voice: "It is me, silly old Owl. Will you please fly to the Castle and tell Maya that I am stuck in this deep dark old rabbit hole? She is the onliest one who can get me out of here."

And of course, Hoot The Owl, with his superior attitude had to ask more questions and show his importance by giving Grampy Poo his advice. "How did you get down there?" he asked.

Now Grampy Poo was getting very irritated with Hoot The Owl, but he said very softly, "I do believe Rabbit dug this hole to trap a bear and he sure caught one--me. Please, Hoot The Owl, go find Maya and tell her of my predicament. Hurry, because it is dark and cold down here."

But Hoot The Owl persisted. "Did you know that in the deep dark jungles of China, the rabbits catch Panda Bears by digging deep dark holes so they will fall in and can't get out?"

Grampy Poo pleaded with Hoot The Owl, "I am stuck down here and I am not a Panda, I am a Grampy Poo."

Suddenly another of Maya's friends, an old Yellow Tiger bounced up, and he bounced right in to the deep dark rabbit hole with Grampy Poo. "Well helllllloooo, there Grampy Poo," said Tellow theTiger (everyone called him Tellow because he was a Tiger and he was yellow). "And how did you get into this deep dark old rabbit hole?"

Grampy Poo was really getting exasperated with Hoot The Owl and Tellow The Tiger, but he was very cool and calm when he said, "Will one of you please go tell Maya where I am and she will come and get me out?"

With that, Hoot The Owl, who thought he was being ignored, said, "Well, why didn't you say so before I went to all the trouble telling you about the Panda Bears in China?" And with that he flew off in the direction of The Enchanted Castle.

Meanwhile down in The Deep Dark Rabbit Hole, Tellow The Tiger was trying to bounce Grampy Poo out but he just didn't have enough bounce.

4

Tellow The Tiger gave up and bouncing out of The Deep Dark Rabbit Hole went bouncing down the path toward the Enchanted Castle to tell Maya of Grampy Poo's dilemma, for he knew that only Maya could figure out how to get him out of that Deep Dark Rabbit Hole.

Meanwhile, Hoot The Owl flew up to Maya's window in The Enchanted Castle and began hooting! "Whooooooo, Whoooooo," he said as he flapped his big old wings.

Maya ran to the window and threw up the sash with such a rush that she almost knocked her old friend Hoot The Owl off the window sill. "What are you doing out there, Owl?" she said. "Come in and I will make some tea and we can have a tea party."

So Hoot The Owl forgot all about Grampy Poo and sat down with his cup of tea. He was having such a good time and he began to tell Maya the story about rabbits in China trapping Panda Bears when who should bounce up but Tellow The Tiger.

" Hi, old buddy boy," he said to Hoot The Owl and Hoot was disappointed because he was only on

5

the third chapter of his story and he had at least ten more chapters in mind, but now he fell silent.

"Hello Tellow," Maya said, "And what brings you to the Enchanted Castle this bright and shiny day?"

Tellow thought and thought and thought but all that bouncing along the path to The Enchanted Castle had shaken his memory buttons and he couldn't remember why he had bounced all this way. So he sat down on a pillow and had a cup of tea with Hoot The Owl and Maya.

Suddenly Maya's friend Rabbit came bounding up the path shouting, "Maya, Maya, Grampy Poo has fallen into my Deep Dark Rabbit hole that I dug to catch Panda Bears and he can't get out."

"Oh my," said Hoot The Owl, "That is what I came to tell you but the tea was so good, I forgot."

Tellow The Tiger bounced up and down and said, "That's what I couldn't remember. I remembers my rememberances now. Grampy Poo is stuck down a rabbit hole just like a Panda Bear in China, but he says he is

not a Panda Bear and this is not China. He is a Grampy Poo. This is America and The Enchanted Forest."

Maya jumped up and ran from the Castle as fast as her little legs would carry her, for her best friend ever-- Grampy Poo--was stuck in a Deep Dark Rabbit Hole in the Enchanted Forest. She knew that she was the only one in the world who could get him out.

When Maya reached the Deep Dark Rabbit Hole, she looked down in but all she could see was dark. However she heard a rumble coming up out of the dark old hole: Snorrrt, snorrrt.....snorrrrt. "Oh my," she said, "has a Buffalump got old Grampy Poo in this Deep Dark Rabbit Hole?" She yelled down into the dark old hole: "Grampy Poo, are you down there?"

The rumbling stopped and up came this voice from the dark old hole. "Hi Maya. This is Grampy Poo, and I am stuck down in this Deep Dark Old Rabbit Hole. Will you get me out please?"

Maya turned to Hoot The Owl and said, "Hoot, please go to Wal-Mart and get me six balloons. You must be careful though or they will carry you away. Have the people at Wal-Mart tie them to Tellow The Tiger's tail and that will hold them down while it will also keep his tail in the air so he cannot bounce, for if he began bouncing with all those balloons he may bounce over the moon."

Everyone laughed except Grampy Poo who was getting very tired of being in this big old Deep Dark Rabbit Hole.

Soon Hoot The Owl came back leading Tellow The Tiger with six balloons tied to his tail. "Here we are buddy boy," shouted Tellow. "Now how do we get Grampy Poo out of this Deep Dark Rabbit Hole?"

Maya said, "Tellow, you have the balloons tied to your tail so that you can't bounce. But you can float, so jump into the big old Deep Dark Rabbit Hole and tie the balloons to Grampy Poo. As he floats up out of the Deep Dark Rabbit Hole, we will catch him so he won't fly away over the moon."

Tellow had already been down in the Deep Dark Rabbit Hole with Grampy Poo so he wasn't afraid to jump in again, but can you guess how Tellow floated down? With the balloons tied to his tail he floated down

head first into the Deep Dark Rabbit Hole.

When Tellow reached the bottom he found Grampy Poo very very, ready to get up and out of the Deep Dark Rabbit Hole.

They tied the balloon string around Grampy Poo and he began to float up, up, up, out of the Deep Dark Rabbit Hole. Faster and faster he went until he reached the top. There Maya reached out and grabbed him by the foot and pulled him safely to the ground outside the Deep Dark Rabbit Hole. Then they untied the balloons from Grampy Poo and let them float away to the moon.

Tellow The Tiger came bouncing out of the Deep Dark Rabbit Hole with a Boing...Boing...Boing.

It was getting dark in the Enchanted Forest so Maya asked all her pretend friends to come to her castle for a sleep over and a tea party.

After the tea party and sleep over at Maya's castle, all the friends said good-bye and went traipsing down the path to the Enchanted Forest. All except Tellow that is.

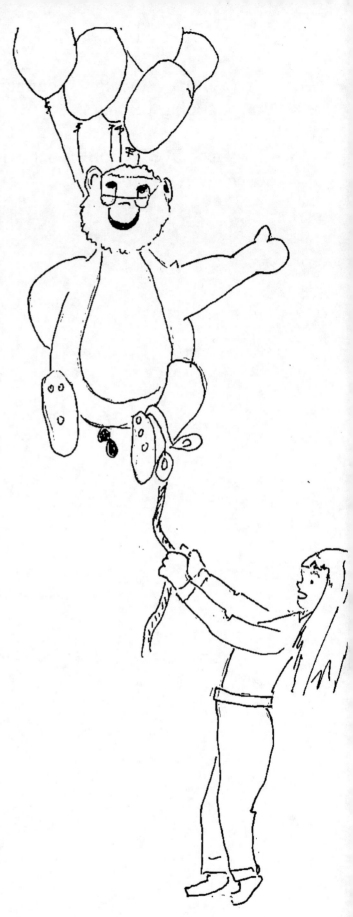

9

Tellow went bouncing:
Boing....Boing....Boing...

Good-bye. Until our next
adventure.

Chapter Two

The Story Of Maya From China And The Dauphin Island Woods

Once upon a time in the Dauphin Island Woods there lived a little girl named Maya. Now Maya was a newcomer to the forest since she had been sent there by The Good Fairy from China to help all the animals who were lost after their best friend Christopher Sparrow went away to school. You see, the Dauphin Island Woods was really an island in the ocean and to attend school, a person had to take the ferry to the mainland and then go to live with a friend until school was out in the spring of the next year. By this time the flowers were blooming, the grass was growing and the birds eggs were hatching. When Maya arrived she found all the pretend animals very sad that they were not going to see their friend, Christopher Sparrow, for what seemed to them to be a very long time.

The Good Fairy Of The Orient had picked Maya from all of the other little children in China to come to the Dauphin Island Woods because she had been blessed with the Power Of The Magic Kiss. Now the Magic Kiss was very powerful

and had been known to do wonderful things such as: turning a frog into a prince or a troll into a frog. But there were other wonders in store for the animals in the forest because even Maya didn't know all the Power Of The Magic Kiss. You see, she had been blessed with it when the Good Fairy whisked her off, issued her a green card and sat her on a rock right in the middle of The Dauphin Island Woods.

Maya was sitting on the rock admiring all the beauty of the forest when who should come slowly down the path but a silly looking old yellow bear wearing a red shirt. Now who could this be, she wondered?

As Maya sat there wondering who this silly old bear was, the rock she sat on began to tremble.

The silly old yellow bear grabbed her and pulled her into the nearby bushes. "Shhhhhh," he said, "It's a Buffalump." Soon the rock stopped rocking and the birds started singing again and the silly old bear held out his hand as though to shake Maya's hand. "Hello," he said, "I am

Gumpy the Bear, and who might you be?"

Maya was quick to reply, "Mister Gumpy the Bear, you have a honey pot stuck on your hand, but I am Maya, most recently of China and I have been sent here by the Good Fairy to cheer up all the pretend animals in the Dauphin Island Woods with my Power of The Pestering and The Power Of The Magic Kiss and what is a Buffalump, if I may ask?"

Gumpy The Bear was so busy trying to pull his hand out of the honey pot that he did not hear a thing Maya had said. Suddenly there was a Schuuucheeee and off slipped the honey pot. With this, Gumpy The Bear spoke while slurping the honey off his hand, "What is your name and where did you come from?" To this Maya retorted with a smile, "I just told you, silly old bear. My name is Maya and I am recently from China. I was sent here by the Good Fairy to cheer up all the pretend animals in the Dauphin Island Woods with my Power of The Pestering and Power of The Magic

14

Kiss. Oh yes, and what is a Buffalump?"

"Oh blooper," said Gumpy The Bear, "All of the animals in the Dauphin Island Woods are very sad because we have lost our very bestest friend ever, Christopher Sparrow, to that silly old school on the mainland and he will not return until school is out. How can anyone help us? My friend Tellow the Tiger has forgotten how to bounce, Rabbit won't dig holes, Hoot The Owl just sits and cries, Whoooooo, all day long and Dink The Donkey won't leave his thistle patch."

To all of this sadness Maya replied, "Silly old Bear, all humans must go to school so they can learn to read, write, and count. It is not necessary for pretend animals to go to school because no one will notice or care if they can't read, spell, or count because they are only pretend, but all children must attend school in order to learn how to speak to animals and play pretend games. Why we wouldn't even be able to have a pretend tea party without school teaching us how to set the

15

table and to make tea. And oh yes, what is a Buffalump, if I may ask?"

Gumpy the Bear just sat there on the rock with his head bowed low and mumbled, "The onliest thing that I know is, when my tummy begins to rumbly, It needs some honey. Who needs to know how to spell hunny when there is so much of it in the Dauphin Island Woods. And we don't need to write because we see each other every day and who needs to count when we have one of everything? Buffalump? how should I know, no one has every seen one."

Maya smiled and said, "Come along, silly old bear and we will visit all your friends and then I can explain to them why humans must attend school." And with that the two new friends tippy-toed, hand in hand through the forest singing, "Twinkle Twinkle Little Star, How I Wonder What You Are?"

Just then Maya leaned down and planted a Magic Kiss on the old bear's beezer and, Wow, Alakazam, Bingo, Bango, Bongo--The silly old bear began to smile and once again

16

he was happy. That was the Power of the Magic Kiss.

They were right in the middle of the second chorus of Twinkle Twinkle Little Star, when who should they see on the path but old Tellow The Tiger. However, he was not bouncing or smiling as he always was but was very sad. Maya said to him, "What is your name, silly old Tiger and why are you so sad?" Tellow replied in a very sad voice, "My name is Tellow The Tiger, spelled with a T double lllloh, and who cares, without Christopher Sparrow, nothing is important anymore. I think I will go live in the thistle patch with Dink The Donkey."

In the blink of an eye, Maya reached out and kissed old Tellow on the beezer and he jumped sky high. Boing, Boing, Boing, he went bouncing as high as the trees and all around the forest. When he came back to the spot where Gumpy The Bear and Maya were standing, he said, "WOWEEEEE, whatever was that? It was like someone hit me on the beezer with a happy stick. I have

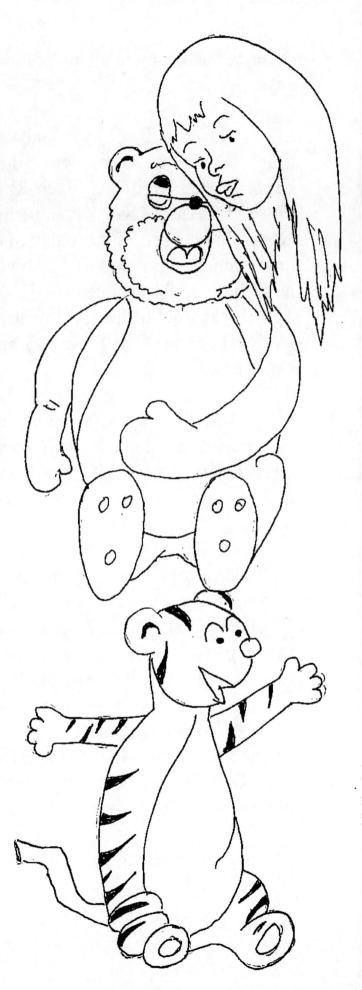

17

never felt so happy in all my borned days."

Maya said, "It was only a Magic Kiss, bestowed on your beezer by me who was given The Power Of The Magic Kiss by the Good Fairy when she brought me here from China. Now if you will help me, possibly we can get Dink The Donkey out of the thistle patch so that I can use The Power on his old beezer."

Tellow said, "Old Dink has been buried in that thistle patch since Christopher Sparrow left for school and I don't believe anyone or anything can pry him out."

Maya said, "You forgot that I also have The Power Of The Pester. I believe I can get him out of the thistle patch." With that, the friends all marched off to the thistle patch.

When the friends arrived at the thistle patch, they found old Hoot The Owl perched on a tree limb above the thistle patch crying, "Whooooo...... Whooooo," and Maya interrupted saying, "Silly old

Owl, please come down here so that I may bestow the Magic Kiss on your old beezer."

Owls, as everyone knows, think they know everything and he began to tell his friends everything he knew and went on and on as owls do. He told about his ancestors who lived with the Panda Bears in China and his cousin who played the drums for George Washington as he marched to the Potomac and started to tell about another of his ancestors when Maya interrupted, "Owl," she said "If you will please fly down here and let me plant a Magic Kiss on your old beezer, I promise that we will tell you who is in the thistle patch."

Hoot The Owl thought very long and very hard about this, but finally his curiosity got the best of him and he plopped down beside Maya on the ground. Before you could blink an eye, she planted a smooch on his old beezer. "Whoooo ooooooooooooooooo...Whoooooooo!" he was heard to exclaim as his wings flapped and he did loop-de-loops in the air crying, "Whooooo, Whooooooo,Whoooooooeeeeeeeeeee."

Now Hoot The Owl was as happy as his friends.

It was now time for the friends to call Dink the Donkey out of the thistle patch and they all began to call: "Dink, oh Dink, oh Dink the Donkey," louder and louder until finally Rabbit came out of the thistle patch and said, "Why are you making so much noise? You are interrupting our pity party. I came here to live in the thistle patch with Dink when Christopher Sparrow went off to school and we don't need company at our pity party. Go away."

Maya said, "If you and Dink the Donkey don't come out of the thistle patch this instant, I will put my Power Of The Pester on you and you will be sorry. I use The Power Of The Pester on my Grampa and he cannot even read his newspaper. Sooooo, I will count to ten and you had better come out or else, Pester, Pester, Pester."

With that Dink The Donkey and the silly old Rabbit scurried out of the thistle patch. Dink said, "I

20

heard about the Power Of The Pester from Grampa and it is almost as bad as a Buffalump. Please don't put it on us little girl. By the way, who are you?"

And Maya said for the umpteenth time, "My name is Maya and I have been sent here by the Good Fairy to cheer up all the pretend animals in the Dauphin Island Woods since Christopher Sparrow has left for school. I have been blessed with The Power Of The Magic Kiss and The Power Of The Pester. If you will all just gather around me I will demonstrate for you." And with this all the animals crowded around her.

Maya demonstrated by placing a Magic Kiss on old Dink The Donkey's soft old beezer and even the old rain clouds went away. Dink galloped and jumped around almost as high as old Tellow and he said, "I feel so good, I don't even want to eat worms, and I will never go back into that old thistle patch again."

Rabbit smiled and smiled, because his old friend Dink was so happy and it made him happy also so Maya didn't have to smooch him on the beezer, he was already so happy.

Maya explained to all the pretend animals, "Christopher Sparrow is a little boy and he is a human. You are all his very best friends ever, but you are really only pretend so it is not necessary for you to learn things like reading, writing and counting, but he must. Some day Christopher Sparrow will be all grown up and live in the real world where he will have grown up friends and they will read, write and count together. But no matter how grown up he gets, he will always remember all his pretend friends in the Dauphin Island Woods."

With that, Maya bid her new friends good-bye and when the Good Fairy came to pick her up, she asked, "Could I stop over at Grampa's house for the weekend?" And the Good Fairy said, "Of course you may. Possibly you can plant a Magic Kiss on his old beezer and make him smile also."

And with that they flew away to Grampa's house and he was so happy to see Maya again that he jumped in the air like old Tellow The Tiger and cried out like Hoot, The Owl, "Whoooooooeeeee, whoooeee!"

Good-bye for now. Until the next adventure.

Chapter Three

Fairy Princess Ling Ling Fo Chi Mon, Maya Lewellyndowski And The Story Of The Magic Ballerina Shoes

Once upon a time in a far away place, clear around on the other side of the globe there was a Fairy Princess named, Ling Ling Fo Chi Mon Maya Lewellyndowski. She was in charge of the Magic Ballerina Slippers. Anyone who wore these slippers at once became an excellent ballerina.

The little Princess loved her name but one day she said to her boss the Princess in charge, "I love my name but it is like saying the alphabet every time someone asks me my name. Soooooo I am going to be known only as Maya from this day forward."

The head Princess said, "Well Maya, I guess that will be okay but what if the boss sends you to America to The Dauphin Island Woods to teach all the animals and pretend creatures there to dance the Ballerina?"

To this Maya replied, "Oh that will never happen because there is a Boy in the Dauphin Island Woods named Christopher Sparrow and he

takes care of all the pretend chores."

And these words had just left her little mouth when, guess what? Well, the big boss Princess came floating in on a cloud from the Magic Palace where she lived and said, "Maya, I want you to fly away with me to The Dauphin Island Woods in America and teach all the pretend animals there how to dance the Ballerina."

To this Maya replied, "My goodness, isn't that what the boy Christopher Sparrow is for?"

The Big Boss Princess looked dismayed as she retorted: "Maya, yours is not to ask why, but why not. Besides, everyone knows Christopher Sparrow is a boy, and what can boys do? Throw rocks, climb trees, play in the mud and all those boy things. We need a little girl to teach these pretend animals a thing or two about dancing, so you must go since you are the keeper of the Magic Ballerina Shoes."

To this Maya replied, "Well I will be happy to go because then I

can visit my Grampa who lives near The Dauphin Island Woods."

No sooner than those words had left Maya's mouth than, BINGO, BANGO, BONGO, ALICAZAM and a FLASH IN THE PAN, and there she was sitting in the middle of The Dauphin Island Woods. She found herself looking up at a large Oak tree and at the very top was a silly looking old bear eating honey out of a bee hive in the tree.

She called, "Silly old bear, come down from that tree and I will teach you the Ballerina Dance as I am the Keeper Of The Magic Ballerina Shoes."

A bee stung the bear on the beezer and he fell out of the tree, landing at Maya's feet. "See here," he said, as he licked the honey from his paw. "I am Gumpy The Bear, And who might you be?"

Maya replied, "Silly old bear. I just told you, I am Maya, Keeper of the Magic Ballerina Shoes, and I want to teach you and the other

pretend animals how to dance the Ballerina." To this Gumpy The Bear cried, "Well, whoop tee doooooo...strap em on me and watch me go to town as the bestest dancer in The Dauphin Island Woods."

Well, with this Maya just smiled and leaning way over she tied the Magic Ballerina Shoes onto the two big old fat legs of her friend, Gumpy The Bear, and--Alakzam, Shinamaroosh and a bolt of lightning--and that fat old bear was spinning around and around doing an alamandar and a sashaaa to the right and a triple lutz. As he had said, he was the bestest Ballerina in the whole wide Dauphin Island Woods.

When Gumpy The Bear finally stopped spinning and twirling around he fell on the ground at Maya's feet and all out of breath said, "Woweeeee, what happened to me? I could never dance. All I could do was climb trees and eat honey."

Maya replied, "See, I told you I was the Keeper Of The Magic Ballerina Shoes and that I could

teach you to dance the Ballerina, you silly old bear." And with that said the two new friends sat on a log and laughed and laughed.

As they were laughing and eating honey, they heard a strange sound coming their way from inside the tree lined forest: Boing...Boing....Boing....went the sound.

This sound startled Maya as it was new to her little ears. "What is that strange noise I hear? It sounds like, Boing.... Boing....Boing."

With that, Gumpy The Bear hugged his tummy and laughed and laughed. "That is silly old Tellow coming up the path." he said and he went on to explain to Maya, "That is just old Tellow. All he ever does is bounce and bounce. Some times he even bounces into Dink The Donkey's thistle patch and we have to pull him out."

And up bounced Tellow. "Hi buddy boy," he said to Gumpy The Bear and then he turned to Maya and said, "Who might you be little

29

girl? You look like a little Chinese Princess I once met in The Dauphin Island Woods when Grampa was stuck down in a Deep Dark Rabbit Hole."

"That is I," said Maya, with a twinkle in her eye. "I have recently been promoted to the Keeper of The Magic Ballerina Shoes. Would you like to learn the Ballerina dance so that you could do something besides bounce all the time?"

"Would I?" said the silly old Tellow. "Just tie em on me and turn me loose."

With that, Maya tied the Magic Ballerina shoes on the silly old Tellow and--Swoooosh, and Ali-Kazaaam with a Filacadush and a Shinamaroosh--Tellow began to glide around the forest. He performed a perfect twinkle toe loop and with his finger on his head he did a perfect kow tow.

Everyone was so busy watching Tellow that they didn't see old Owl fly up and land quietly on the grass behind all the friends.

30

"What is this?" demanded the old bird who thought he knew everything. Now everyone knows that Owls are very smart, but this old Owl just loved to tell all his friends how smart he was, sooooo he began making a speech about the Panda Bears in China and he went on and on. Maya interrupted his speech and said, "Mister Owl, would you like to learn to dance the Ballerina dance like Tellow?" And Owl replied in the affirmative. Owl was the greatest, because with his big old wings he could twirl and then take off and fly. He triple-toe looped and curtsied all over the forest. "Whoooooooooeeeeee," Owl could be heard shouting all over the forest.

All this noise and clatter could be heard clear to Grampa's house and when he heard it he came running as fast as he could on his little old legs.

Grampa screeched to a halt and said, "What's going on here? I can hear you clear down on Dauphin Island."

Maya stepped up to Grampa and gave him a big hug and a kiss on the Beezer. She said to him. "Grampa, the Good Fairy has promoted me to be The Keeper of The Magic Ballerina Shoes and I have been sent here to teach everyone the Ballerina Dance. Would you like to learn the dance?"

Grampa said, "Maya, honey, I love you with all my heart but you know I can't dance a lick. I can't do the swim because I'm too thin and I can't do the waltz because I'm too smaltz, so you see honey I am a hopeless case." With this said, Grampa hung his head and started to walk away down the path.

Maya shouted, "Wait Grampa, let me put the Magic Ballerina Shoes on your feet and you will see. You will be a great dancer just like Gumpy The Bear, Owl, and Tellow. Just try it."

Grampa sat down on a rock and Maya tied the Magic Ballerina Shoes on his feet and....Wow he became the star dancer of the forest.

After Grampa had waltzed around the forest several times, he sat down next to Maya on a rock and she said, "See, I told you so." And with that, they all held hands and skipped through the forest to Grampa's house and had a Tea Party.

It was a wonderful day.

Goodbye, until the next adventure.

Chapter Four

Maya and Gumpy Boo

Once upon a time in an Enchanted Forest their lived an old yellow bear. Everyone called him Boo.

Now everyone knows that a Boo is a bear and a Grumpy is an old Grump, so his real name was Grumpy Boo.

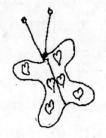

He lived in a gloomy place where the sun didn't shine and under a dark wet cloud and this cloud followed him everywhere he went. It was a very gloomy place and all anyone ever heard him say was, "Bah, Humbug."

Not far away in the sunny side of the forest lived a little girl named Maya. Maya had been sent to the forest by the Good Fairy, to make everyone smile and to teach them how to be happy.

Maya had been blessed with The Power Of The Magic Kiss by the Good Fairy. This was a special kiss to be used only in extreme cases. She could kiss a frog and turn him into a Prince or a Troll and turn

him into a frog, but she had never kissed a Grumpy Boo.

One day Maya was talking to her good friend, Hoot The Owl, when it slipped out of owl's mouth that there was a Grumpy Boo living in the Enchanted Forest. Owl told Maya that every one was afraid of the Grumpy Boo because he was so grumpy. It just slipped out, because as everyone knows, owls love to talk.

Maya said, "What's a Grumpy Boo, Owl, and why does he scare all of the people and animals in the Enchanted Forest?"

Owl, being so wise and loving to talk, replied, "Well, everyone knows that a Boo is an old bear and a Grumpy is an old Grump, so Voila, a Grumpy Boo is a Grumpy Old Bear." I suppose everyone is afraid of him because he is so grumpy....All he ever says is, "Bah, Humbug."

Owl wanted to go on and talk, talk, talk, but Maya stopped him by repeating what Owl had said. "A

BAH HUMBUG

grumpy old Bear. Why is he grumpy? Is he sick? Is he tired? Is he lonesome?" And to each of these questions, Owl nodded knowingly "Whooooooo, Whooooooo...," he said.

Maya being the good person she was and also just a little curious, having never seen a Grumpy Boo, wanted to set out at once for the gloomy side of the forest in search of it.

Owl was still talking and didn't see Maya leave as she tippy-toed through the woods searching for a Grumpy Boo.

As Maya tippy-toed through the forest, she soon came to a gloomy place with a dark old wet cloud hanging over it and an old gloomy donkey sitting under the cloud getting all wet. It was Dink The Donkey.

Maya spoke to Dink The Donkey in a very nice happy voice. "Dink," she said, "Have you seen a Grumpy Boo in the Enchanted Forest?" Dink replied in a gloomy voice, "No Maya, I haven't seen a Grumpy Boo. Why would it be in my thistle patch?"

Maya said, "Owl told me he was an old bear who was very grumpy and he lives under a cloud in a thistle patch. I thought you might know him."

Dink spoke again as he turned to walk away, "Well, I don't even know what a Grumpy Boo is but if you find one and he lives under a leaky cloud in a thistle patch like I do, he would probably be just like me. Oh well, nothing ever gets any better. I think I will go eat worms."

Maya continued on her quest to find a Grumpy Boo as she went deeper and deeper into the forest.

As she tippy-toed through the deep dark forest, she came upon a little river with a tiny bridge crossing it. Under the bridge lived an ugly old Troll who collected a toll from all who crossed.

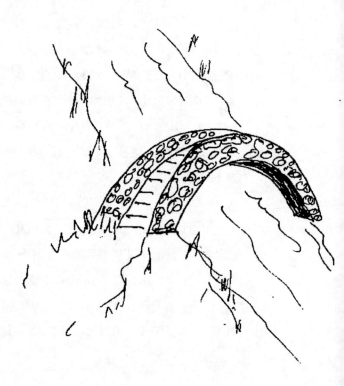

The ugly old Troll jumped out onto the bridge and shouted at

Maya, "I know who you are. You are Maya, the little girl who can kiss a frog and turn him into a Prince. If you kiss me, I will turn into a giant, so your toll to cross the bridge is one Magic Kiss. If you don't do what I demand, you will never find your Grumpy Boo."

Maya thought and thought, but she didn't know what to do. Suddenly there was a flash and the Good Fairy appeared before her eyes. The Good Fairy said to Maya, "Do not worry Maya, if he is sure that is what he wants, go ahead and kiss him on the head and see what happens."

So Maya being the sweet little girl that she is, leaned over and planted a Magic Kiss on the old Troll's head. Bingo, Bango, Bongo, a flash, and where the Ugly Old Troll once stood was a big old green frog. "Croak, croak, croak," was all he could say.

Wouldn't you know, the Magic Kiss only works for good people and animals and it works just backwards for bad people and Trolls. That is why the Ugly Old Troll, turned into a green frog.

And so Maya continued over the river and through the woods in search of the Grumpy Boo's house.

As she tippy-toed through the forest, she grew very hungry. She was looking around for a sandwich and french fries, when all of a sudden she heard, "Harrrummmmph....Harrrummmmm mmph."

The sound frightened her just a little but she remembered that this was the Enchanted Forest and nothing bad could ever happen to her here. So she looked and looked to see where the sound came from.

"Harrummmmmmph................. Harrmmmmmmph." There it was again. It seemed to come from those bushes over there. Maya walked over to the bushes and pulled them apart. Guess what was hiding in the bushes?

Behind the bushes stood an old grumpy looking bear and once again

40

he said, "Harruuuuuumph." Then he said, "Bah Humbug." Maya knew in an instant that she had found the Grumpy Boo she had been searching for.

Maya said to him, " You must be the Grumpy Boo because you are an old bear and you sure are grumpy." With that, the old bear came out of the bushes, which were really a thistle patch and his little black, leaky, wet cloud followed him.

"Yes" he said, "I am a Grumpy Boo and you would be grumpy also if you had no friends and this old black leaky cloud hung over you all the time."

Maya took his hand and said, "I can make it all better for you since I have been given the Power Of The Magic Kiss. May I plant one on your old beezer?"

The Grumpy Boo said, "Kiss....Shmiss...What good will a little kiss do a grumpy old bear?" And with this he turned to walk back into the thistle patch.

41

Maya shouted, "Wait...Wait," and she ran over to him and planted a big old Magic Kiss on his old beezer. Flash...Bam...Boom...Ali...... Kazam!

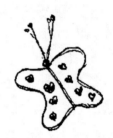

Where the grumpy old bear once stood was a smiling old fat bear and the black leaky cloud was gone. They looked, and the thistle patch had turned into a beautiful little house and garden with the sun shining on it and flowers blooming everywhere.

Maya said, "See, I told you, didn't I?" Now all the animals in the Enchanted Forest laughed and cheered. They named the happy old bear, Grampy Boo and that is how Grampy Boo was born in the Enchanted Forest.

Everyone was very happy so they all went to Grampy Boo's new beautiful house and had a tea party.

Good-bye for now, until the next adventure.

Chapter Five

The Story Of Maya
And The Power Of The Magic Eye

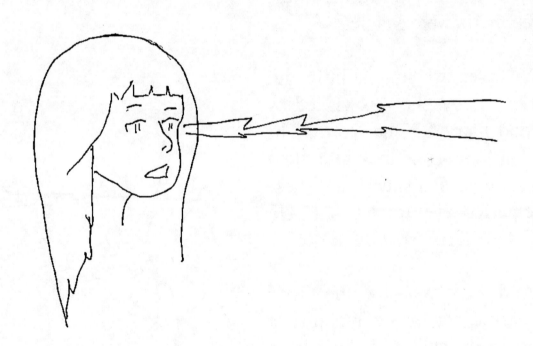

O nce upon a time in a land far-far away there was a little girl born with two great big black eyes. Her eyes were so big and black that it seemed like you could just jump in them and get lost.

There was, however, a great difference between these eyes and the eyes of all the other little children: her's were Magic.

You see when this little girl was a tiny baby, she was visited by the Good Fairy Of The North. The Good Fairy took one look into those big black eyes and she said, "These are the perfect eyes to be given THE POWER OF THE MAGIC EYE."

And so it was that the Good Fairy passed her Magic Wand over the tiny baby and said the Magic Words, Alakazaaam, Shinamaringding..this little baby shall have the Power Of The Magic Eye thing."And with that it was done.

The Good Fairy explained that her Gramma would have to watch

the baby very closely until she gets to be five years old. If she happened to wink at the wrong person she could cause them to fall in love, fall out of love, turn into a frog, turn into a prince or princess or just become a lump on a log.

She said, "Gramma, This little child will not know the power within her eye until she is five years old and you will have to keep her from winking until then. If she accidently winks at someone in Wal-Mart they could turn into a potato or even a grocery basket. So watch her very closely and control her wink."

The years passed very quickly and the baby grew to be a big girl and they had only one winking accident. At one time when she was three the little girl got something in her eye and she blinked. Now a blink is not a wink, everyone knows that, but the poor dog who got in the way of the blink turned into a kitten.

Gramma said, "Now isn't that a fine howdy dooo?" She said to the child, "Try blinking the other eye at

the kitten and see what happens."
And the little girl blinked her left
eye and the kitten turned back into a
dog.

The dog said, "Now why did
you do that? I was liking being a
kitten. Can you turn me back?" So
the little girl blinked her right eye
and the dog turned back into a
kitten. "Meoooow," she said and ran
off down the aisle at Wal-Mart and
disappeared into the crowd, a very
happy little cat.

This all happened when the
little girl was three years old and
there were no more accidents until
on her fifth birthday. It was on this
day that the Good Fairy appeared at
the party and explained to the little
girl The Power Of The Magic Eye.

Can you guess who the little
girl is? If you guessed Maya, you are
right.

The Good Fairy said to Maya,
"Maya, you are my favorite little girl
in all the world. That is why I gave
you the POWER OF THE MAGIC
EYE. You are a kind and sweet little

46

girl and I know you will use the Power only for good, but you must remember you cannot wink at the little boys because you could turn them into a Wal-Mart cart. Just remember one thing. Your right eye does all the damage and if you wink your left eye you can undo what your right eye has done and put everything back as it was. So now be off with you and make bad things turn to good with your Power Of The Magic Eye."

The very next day Maya came to Dauphin Island to visit her Grampa and she forgot to tell him about The Power Of The Magic Eye until it was too late.

As they were walking through the parking lot headed for the China Doll for lunch with Maya on Grampa's shoulders, Maya looked down and winked her right eye--and Bingo, Bango, Bongo, right there in the parking lot, Grampa turned into a mouse.

Now everyone laughed to see this little girl riding on the shoulders of a mouse.

47

Everyone laughed, except Grampa, that is. From way down on the ground in the parking lot came this little squeaky mouse voice and it was saying, "Maya, what did you do? Look at me, I am a little bitty mouse and if you don't put me back like I was, you will have to put me in your pocket and carry me in to the China Doll. But they won't let a mouse eat in there and how can I drive the car to take us home?"

Maya just laughed and laughed. "Grampa," she said, "I was just practicing the Power Of The Magic Eye. I can put you back like you were, don't worry." Then she began to explain the Power Of The Magic Eye to Grampa and he just squeaked, "Put me back, put me back, and then tell all about it."

Maya said, "Okey dokey," and she winked her left eye at Grampa and Wow, Alykazam, he turned from a mouse to the same old guy with a white mustache and a little five year old girl on his shoulders.

As they went on into the China Doll Grampa said, "If you ever do

48

that again Maya, please make me into something big like a horse or an elephant so that I can carry you on my shoulders," Then they both laughed and laughed as they were seated in the China Doll to eat Rangoons.

The next day was Saturday and Maya decided to go to the Dauphin Island Woods to see all the pretend animals and practice the Power Of The Magic Eye on them. She thought, "I would like to change old Tellow into a chicken. I'll bet that would stop his bouncing."

So off she went tippy toeing into the Dauphin Island Woods and who should she meet on the path but old Tellow and he was bouncing-- boing, boing, boing, boing. Maya said, "If you don't stand still and stop that boinging I am going to turn you into a chicken."

Tellow answered with another boing and said, " Maya, I know you have the Power Of The Magic Kiss and the Magic Ballerina Shoes, but turn me into a chicken? I don't think so."

49

With that said, Maya just winked her eye and Alakazam, Bingo, Bango, Bongo, and a flash in the pan and there stood an old chicken where Tellow once stood, boinging and boinging.

Old Tellow squawked in his new chicken voice, "Maya, Maya, what have you done? Can you turn me back into a Tellow? If you do I promise to always believe you and I will not boing anymore when you ask me to stop."

With that Maya just winked her left eye and old Tellow became himself again.

Tellow said, "Boy oh boy, you really can change things with your Power Of The Magic Eye. Do you suppose you could change the old Troll at the bridge into a pig? That would be real funny and it might teach him a lesson."

Maya said, "Okey, dokey, but I am not supposed to use my power just to have fun. I do think that old Troll needs to be taught a lesson, though, for scaring so many people

when they cross the bridge."

So off the two friends went skipping through the woods to the Old Troll Bridge.

As they stepped on the bridge the ugly old Troll jumped out from under and shouted, "Who is that trying to cross my bridge? Don't you know that you have to pay a toll to step on my bridge?"

To that Maya answered, "Mr. Troll, you must stop scaring everyone who crosses this bridge or I shall have to turn you into a pig and let the Big Bad Wolf chase you through the woods."

The ugly old Troll laughed and said, "I know you have the power of the Magic Kiss but no one can turn a Troll into a Pig."

With that Maya just winked and Wham, Bam--a bolt of lightning, a loud squawk and there where the Troll once stood was a pig. The pig squealed and squealed and ran off into the woods with the Big Bad Wolf right behind him.

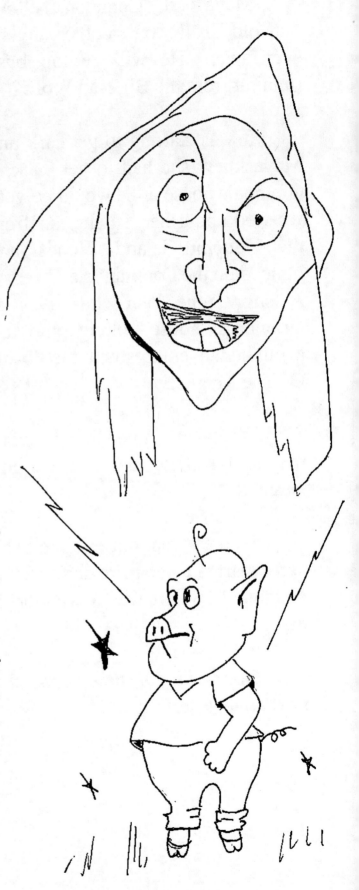

51

Maya said, "Come on, Tellow, that old Troll won't bother anyone ever again. He will be too busy running from the Big Bad Wolf."

It was starting to get dark and Maya knew she had to get back to Grampa's house or he would be very worried about her, so she ran from the Dauphin Island Woods and jumped on the Dauphin Island Ferry. A short time later she was at Grampa's house telling him all about her adventures with the Power Of The Magic Eye.

When Maya told Grampa about the old Troll he just laughed and laughed.

So they went out into the back yard, started a campfire and roasted marshmallows. It was a wonderful day.

Good-bye for now, until the next adventure.

Chapter Six

The Story Of Maya, Grampa, Santa Claus and the Alakazambackaroo... Shinamaroo Carpet

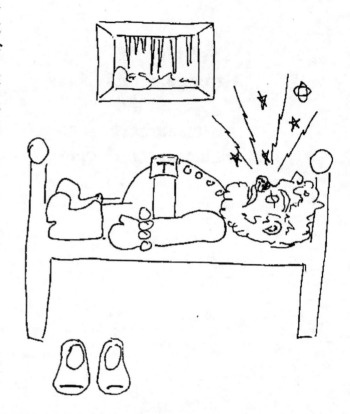

O nce upon a time in a land called the North Pole, far away, just north of China and to the left of America, there lived a jolly old fat man named Santa Claus. Now Santa Claus was blessed with the Magic of Toys. It was his sole purpose in life to load his sleigh with toys on Christmas Eve and deliver them to all the good girls and boys all over the world.

Now it was the day before Christmas and poor old Santa was sick in bed with a terrible cold in his beezer. He moaned and he groaned but to no avail. It looks like for the first time ever Santa will not be able to deliver his toys on the night before Christmas.

All the little elves were rushing around falling down and shouting at each other because Santa was sick and they had no one to lead them.

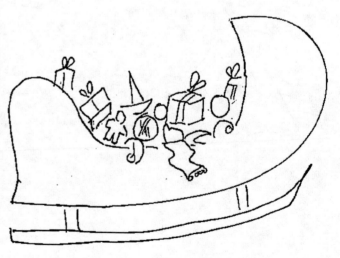

They had the sleigh all loaded with toys but no one knew how to hook up the reindeer. "Oh my! Oh my! What shall we do?" they cried!

All the little elves were beside themselves. They thought, "Shall we unload the sleigh and call UPS? Or maybe we should just take all the packages to the Post Office and mail them."

"No No No," said Mrs. Claus, in a very stern voice, and all the little elves stopped what they were doing and listened to what she had to say because they all knew that Santa was the Big Cheese but Mrs. Santa really ran the show.

Mrs. Santa said to the elves sternly, "We will ask the jolly old fat man what he thinks we should do. You know he has been doing this for a thousand years and has never missed a delivery. He is even better than Fed Ex."

So they all went into Santa's bedroom where he was lying on his bed moaning and groaning and Mrs. Claus said, "Hey, jolly old fat man, what do you want us to do with all these toys?"

"Call Maya!" He shouted. "She is the onliest one who can do this

delivery. Maya has been blessed by the Good Fairy with the Magic Kiss, The Magic Eye, and the Magic Ballerina Shoes so I just know she will find a way to deliver all these toys to the little girls and boys all around the world."

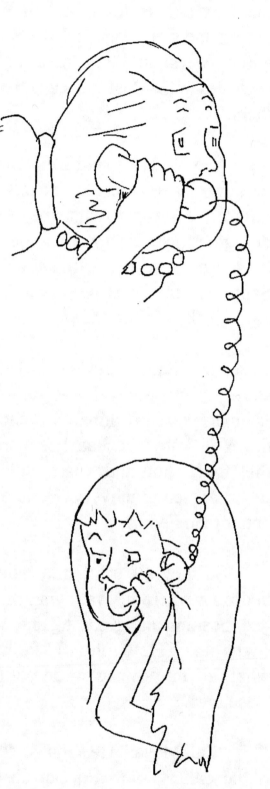

So Mrs. Claus went to her cell phone and dialed, 1-800-Maya. And guess what?

The little voice on the other end of the line came over loud and clear: "Hello, you have reached Maya's residence. What can I do for you?"

Mrs. Claus told Maya the story about Santa Claus with the cold in his beezer and the elves who had loaded the sleigh and that Santa told them to call Maya.

Maya said, "I will use my Magic powers and fly to the North Pole this very instant, but first I have to stop on Dauphin Island to pick up Grampa because he always helps me in these tough cases."

And so away she flew on her Magic Carpet to Dauphin Island

where she picked up Grampa and he complained all the way to the North Pole: "I am afraid to fly. It is too cold. Why me? Why not Christopher Sparrow?"And on and on.

But when they arrived at the North Pole, Maya took charge. First, she went in to see Santa Claus to assure him that the deliveries would be made on time and then she gave him a Magic Kiss on the sore Beezer and went about loading the sleigh and getting Rudolph and all the other reindeer hitched to the sleigh.

"Come on,Grampa,"she said, "Let's get this show on the road. Times a wastin'." So Awaaaaaay they flew into the night.

The first house they came to was in Sturgis and Grampa said, "I know all these little kids, I will climb down these chimneys and deliver all the presents in Sturgis."

Maya said, "I don't think so." But it was too late, Grampa had jumped off the sleigh and into the chimney.

"Oh my goodness," he exclaimed, "I am stuck. I am too fat to get down this chimney and I don't know the Magic word that Santa uses to slide in and...Oh My, I am stuck."

And so it was that Maya uttered the Magic words, (too secret to be printed here), and out popped old Grampa. "Thank you, little girl. I thought I was stuck in there forever. For the rest of the trip, I will hold the reins of the reindeer and give you the packages and you will have to do all the heavy work, especially since you know all the Magic Words."

And so it was, they flew from house to house all around the globe and Maya used the Magic Words to get down the chimneys and Grampa moaned and groaned about the cold.

They were busy the whole night. They visited the Dauphin Island Woods and left gifts for all the pretend animals.

Maya dropped in and out of chimneys all night and because of the Magic Words she never even got her hands dirty. But she was a very tired little girl when they arrived back at the North Pole and tied up Rudolph and all the other reindeer.

Maya went in to see Santa Claus and he was up and chipper again. He said, "That Magic Kiss you planted on my Beezer made me all well again but I surely do thank you for making all my deliveries tonight. May I call on you again if I get into trouble?"

Maya smiled her beautiful smile and said, "Of course you may...but next time we have to leave Grampa home because he is too fat to get down the chimneys. In fact he even got stuck in one last night and I had to use the Magic Words to get him out."

Every one laughed and laughed at the thought of Grampa being stuck up in a chimney. Grampa just groaned..... "Ohhhhhhh."

Maya and Grampa went all around the workshop on the North Pole and said Thank You to all the elves, Mrs. Claus, and of course all the reindeer. It was time for them to leave so they climbed aboard the Magic Carpet and Maya said the M a g i c W o r d s . . . "Alakazambackaroo, Shinamaroo" and off they flew to the Dauphin Island Woods and the last anyone saw of them, they were skipping hand in hand down the path to Gumpy The Bear's house where they had a tea party.

Goodbye for now...until the next adventure.

Epilogue

Who decides to write a children's book and why?

The Adventures Of Maya And Grampa books are a collection of small six or eight page books written and illustrated by me, Grampa, Gampy Poo, Ken Marshall as requested by little Maya who came to us from China as a thirteen month old adoptee.

Maya lived with me pretty much for the period of her life when her adopted mother was very ill and following her death Maya moved to Florida to live with her Grandmother. As she was leaving my house two years ago, June of 2002, she turned and with tears in her eyes said, "Write me a book Grampa," and I of course without thinking I said, "Okay." It then dawned on me that she was only four years old and I seventy five. This being the case I had no clue as to what a four year old thinks about so I asked, "About what?" And she without hesitation replied, "The Power Of The Magic Eye."

Now how in blazes does an old man of seventy five write about The Power Of The Magic Eye when he has not an ounce of knowledge about the subject? So I sat down at my computer and the results are printed in this book. Each of these subjects were chosen by Maya as I would complete one book after the other until I had a great number of them.

I chose to have all the works published in several 60 page books to be presented to Maya when she is much older. You will find that these books, or chapters if you will, are not sequential and are in no order but are part of a collection of the books I wrote for a little four year old Chinese girl. I have several more in the making.

I hope you enjoy reading these books as much as I enjoyed writing them.

Sincerely,

Ken Marshall (Grampa or Grampy Poo)